Dear Parent:
Your child's love of reading starts here!

I Can Read Books have introduced children to the joy of reading since 1957. Featuring award-winning authors and illustrators and a fabulous cast of beloved characters, I Can Read Books set the standard for beginning readers. From books your child reads with you to the first books they read alone, there are I Can Read Books for every stage of reading:

SHARED READING
Basic language, word repetition, and whimsical illustrations, ideal for sharing with your emergent reader

BEGINNING READING
Short sentences, familiar words, and simple concepts for children eager to read on their own

READING WITH HELP
Engaging stories, longer sentences, and language play for developing readers

READING ALONE
Complex plots, challenging vocabulary, and high-interest topics for the independent reader

ADVANCED READING
Short paragraphs, chapters, and exciting themes for the perfect bridge to chapter books

Every child learns in a different way and at their own speed. Some read through each level in order. Others go back and forth between levels and read favorite books again and again. You can help your young reader improve and become more confident by encouraging their own interests and abilities.

A lifetime of discovery begins with the magical words, **"I Can Read!"**

HarperCollins®, ≝®, and I Can Read Book® are trademarks of HarperCollins Publishers Inc.

The Berenstain Bears' New Pup
Printed in the U.S.A. For information address HarperCollins Children's Books,
a division of HarperCollins Publishers, 10 East 53rd Street, New York, NY 10022.
www.harperchildrens.com
Library of Congress Cataloging-in-Publication Data

Berenstain, Stan.
  The Berenstain Bears' new pup / Stan & Jan Berenstain.—1st ed.
      p.   cm. — (An I can read book)
    Summary: Mama, Sister, and Brother are excited about the puppy they bring home from Farmer Ben's farm, even
though she takes a lot of care.
    ISBN 0-06-058344-4 (pbk.)— ISBN 0-06-058343-6
    [1. Pets—Fiction.   2. Dogs—Fiction.   3. Animals—Infancy—Fiction.   4. Responsibility—Fiction.   5. Bears—
Fiction.]   I. Berenstain, Jan.   II. Title.   III. Series.
  PZ7.B4483Bffd   2005   2004006237
  [E]—dc22

Typography by Scott Richards

14 15 16 17 18 LP/WOR 10 9 8
❖
First Edition

I Can Read!™

BEGINNING READING 1

The Berenstain Bears'
New Pup

Stan & Jan Berenstain

HarperCollins*Publishers*

One day Mama and the cubs
went to Farmer Ben's farm.
They went there to buy
some fresh eggs.

"Look!" said Brother. "There is a sign

on Farmer Ben's barn door."

The sign said PUPS FOR SALE!

"Hmm," said Mama.

"Farmer Ben's dog, Queenie,

must have had pups."

"Oh, Mama!" said Sister.

"May we have one? May we?

May we? Please?"

"We came to buy eggs," said Mama.

"Not a pup."

Farmer Ben was in the barn.

So was his dog, Queenie.

Queenie was in a box with her pups.

There were many pups.

Some of her pups were having lunch.

Some were sleeping.

One of them was playing

with a piece of straw.

"Oh," said Sister.

"I want that one!

He is so cute."

"That one is a she," said Farmer Ben.

"How can you tell?" asked Brother.

"There are ways," said Farmer Ben.

"Now, cubs," said Mama,

"buying eggs is one thing.

Buying a pup is quite another."

"Oh, Mama," said the cubs,

"may we have her?

May we? May we? Please?"

"A pup is not just something
you have," said Mama.
"A pup is something
you have to take care of."
"We will take care of her!"
said the cubs.

"A pup is something you have to

clean up after," said Mama.

"We will clean up after her,"

said the cubs.

"A pup likes to get into things,"
said Mama.

"We will watch her every second!"
said the cubs.

Farmer Ben picked up the pup

that was playing with the straw.

He put her in Mama's hands.

The pup looked into Mama's eyes.

The pup licked Mama's nose.

The pup wagged her tail…

and Mama's heart melted!

On the way home,

they named the pup Little Lady.

They named her "little"

because she was little.

They named her "lady"

because she was a she.

"Yum!" said Papa Bear

when they got home.

"A dozen farm-fresh eggs!"

"And one farm-fresh pup!"

said Sister Bear.

Mama was right about Little Lady.

She did have to be cleaned up after.

She left a puddle in one corner…

and a calling card in another.

And she did like to get into things.

She got into Mama's baking flour.

Cough! Cough! Cough!

She got into Papa's fishing tackle.

What a tangle!

She got into Farmer Ben's

farm-fresh eggs.

What a mess!

"Hmm," said Mama.

"I am going back to Farmer Ben's."

"You're not going to take Little Lady

back to Farmer Ben's?" cried Sister.

"No," said Mama.

"I am just going to get another dozen eggs."